Two Little Boys – Ten Big Plagues

Written by Carol Craven Bates

Illustrated by Janet Church Hopkins

Jolly Journey

Publishing

Centerville, Tennessee

ISBN: 978-0-615-28357-9

Printed in the United States of America

To order additional copies of this book, contact:

Jolly Journey Publishing
www.JollyJourneyPublishing.com
sales@JollyJourneyPublishing.com

For everyone who has ever had a dream, I give you Psalm 37:4:

"Delight thyself also in the Lord and He shall give thee the desires of thine heart."

Two Little Boys – Ten Big Plagues is a fictional story based on the true story in the Bible of the ten plagues that God sent on Egypt found in Exodus chapters 7 – 14:

Plague #1 – Water into Blood – Exodus 7:20 - 21

Plague #2 – Frogs – Exodus 8:3-6

Plague #3 – Lice – Exodus 8:16 - 17

Plague #4 – Flies – Exodus 8:24

Plague #5 – Murrain – Exodus 9:3-6

Plague #6 – Boils – Exodus 9:8-10

Plague #7 – Hail – Exodus 9:18 - 24

Plague #8 – Locusts – Exodus 10:4-6

Plague #9 – Darkness – Exodus 10:21 - 22

Plague #10 – Death of the Firstborn – Exodus 12:29

Crossing the Red Sea – Exodus 14:1-31

*Plagues 1-3 affected everyone living in Egypt. Plagues 4-9 affected only the Egyptians. Plague number 10 was the only one that had a condition for avoidance; it affected everyone who didn't do what the Lord required.

In case you are not familiar with the ten plagues of Egypt, this is a brief Bible history to help you understand. These are true statements found in the Bible.

1. Abraham was a chosen man of God.

2. Abraham had a son named Isaac.

3. Isaac had twin sons named Jacob and Esau.

4. Jacob was chosen by God to carry on the family line.

5. God changed Jacob's name to Israel.

   That is where the nation of Israel that we know of today got its name. They were first called Hebrews and later called Israelites.

6. There was a famine in the land where Jacob/Israel lived, so he moved his family to Egypt.

7. Later, after Jacob/Israel died, his family the Israelites became slaves to the Egyptians.

8. The Israelites stayed in Egypt for four hundred and thirty years, living in the part of Egypt called Goshen.

9. God chose a man named Moses to lead the Israelites out of Egyptian slavery.

10. Before the Pharaoh (king) of Egypt would release the Israelites, God had to send ten plagues to get his attention.

11. Finally, God helped Moses lead the Israelites out of Egypt.

12. That was when God parted the Red Sea for the people to escape.

Character List

Hebrew Family
Jalon Grossman - Son
Leah Grossman - Mother
David Grossman - Father

Egyptian Family
Mecho Poriah   - Youngest Son
Zina Poriah   - Daughter
Ketar Poriah   - Oldest Son
Ishca Poriah   - Mother
Ramar Poriah   - Father

Moses   - Brother to Aaron and Miriam
Aaron   - Brother to Moses and Miriam
Miriam   - Sister to Moses and Aaron

Pharaoh   - King of Egypt

Mr. Phalu   - Neighbor/Animal Doctor

Chapter 1

Jalon Grossman and Mecho Poriah were two little boys living in Egypt during the time the Israelites were serving as slaves to the Egyptians. Jalon was born in Egypt, but belonged to a Hebrew family. He was the only child of David and Leah Grossman. The Hebrew people were sometimes referred to as Israelites or the children of Israel.

Mecho was the youngest son of Ramar and Ishca Poriah. He had an older brother, Ketar, and a younger sister, Zina. Mecho and his family were full-fledged Egyptians and related to Pharaoh through ancient ancestry.

Jalon and Mecho met while fishing on the banks of the Nile River. Every day, each boy went to the river as soon as their morning chores were finished and stayed until it was time to do chores again in the evening.

Jalon and Mecho each had their own favorite fishing spot along the Nile, but even though they fished just a few feet apart, they seldom spoke. That all changed one day when Jalon caught a fish that was so large it wouldn't fit in his bucket. Mecho just had to go over and see that glorious sight.

After that, there was always an unspoken bond between the two boys. They soon started communicating much more often, and before long they became the best of friends. They started spending as much time together as they could, generally fishing. Usually Egyptians avoided having Hebrew friends; however, both sets of parents didn't mind the boys being together.

Jalon and Mecho lived a half mile apart, but they would often dash from one house to the other as if they lived just next door. The boys were complete opposites in everything except fishing. In that category, they were pretty evenly matched. They both thought fishing was the only way to have fun. If one boy had chores that took too long to do, the other would help so they could have more time together at the river.

On one occasion, while Jalon and Mecho were spending their afternoon fishing, they started talking about the stranger that had come to town. Both boys had heard their parents discussing the newcomer. The mysterious foreigner was the hottest topic for everyone to talk about. There was a rumor going around that the new man had visited Pharaoh uninvited, which, in itself, was something no one was allowed to do. Besides that, he demanded that Pharaoh let the Israelites leave Egypt so they could worship their God.

The children were intrigued by the bold actions of this mystery man. While Jalon landed the biggest fish he had caught in several days, Mecho stated, "The name of the new guy is Moses. He dresses funny. Mom said that was because he lives in the desert. Dad told us he thought Moses has a brother living around here. His name is Aaron, I think."

Excitedly, Jalon shouted, "Yeah, I know Aaron! He and my dad are friends. He has a sister that lives around here too. Her name is Miriam. I've seen her around, but no one seems to know her very well. I wonder how come Moses lives in the desert when he has family that lives right here?"

Mecho shook his head and shrugged his shoulders, "I have no idea, but my dad said Moses and his brother got into an argument with Pharaoh. Can you believe that? I wonder what they were thinking. That could have been instant death."

This time, it was Mecho who snagged a big fish. "Wow! Look at this guy. I bet this is the biggest fish I ever caught." Jalon helped Mecho get his fish secured on the ground before going back to his own pole. After throwing back a smaller fish and putting the bigger one in his wooden bucket, Mecho snickered, "My dad was telling us that Aaron, the brother of the new guy, threw his walking stick down and it turned into a snake right there in the palace. At first Pharaoh was surprised; then he got mad. He called for his magicians and asked them if they could do that. They didn't want to look bad in front of Pharaoh so they did some of their magic. In a little while they threw down their walking sticks and those became snakes too."

The eyes of Jalon lit up with delight. "Wow! That would be so exciting. I wish we could have seen all those snakes crawling all over the palace."

Mecho continued, "My dad also told us the snake from the rod of Aaron ate up all the other snakes. The funny part was it never even got fatter. When all the other snakes were gone, Aaron reached down and picked his snake up. When he grabbed it by the tail it turned back into a rod again. Man! That would have been so nifty. I sure wish we could have been there."

The boys continued to fish and contemplate all the fun they had missed at the palace until they noticed the sun was going down. As the sun started to set, the boys knew it was time for them to be heading home. Mecho was the first to suggest they meet at the river as early as they could in the morning and fish all day long.

Jalon grinned, "You took the words right out of my mouth, but I can only stay until lunchtime. My mom plans on washing clothes tomorrow, and I always help her empty those heavy clay tubs. Those things are much too heavy for her to handle alone. I can meet you in the morning though. Usually mom isn't finished with the laundry until after lunch. She won't need me before then."

Both boys silently pulled the line of their cane pole out of the water. Mecho picked up his bucket and admired the three fish he had caught. Jalon had caught only two. One of them was almost too small to keep. He suggested Mecho take those as well. Pouring his fish in with the others, Jalon declared, "Okay, I'll see you first thing in the morning." The boys said goodbye and went straight home.

Chapter 2

The sun was barely up the next morning when Jalon arrived at the riverbank. He was carrying his cane fishing pole and two wooden buckets. The smaller bucket was filled to the brim with dough balls. The larger one was empty. Jalon was hoping to fill that one with the fish he caught. To his surprise, Mecho was already there and pulling out his second fish of the day.

Mecho looked over at Jalon and giggled. "You better speed it up, slow poke. They're really hungry this morning. I just barely got my hook in the water until I had a fish on it. Hurry and throw in your line before I catch them all. I sure am glad you thought to bring some more bait. The way the fish are biting, we're going to be out in no time, and we sure don't want to take time to dig for worms."

Excitedly, Jalon took his place on the bank beside Mecho. "I want to show you something. My dad made a brand new fish hook for me last night. He carved it out of a piece of bone from a ram. Dad told me it wouldn't be as strong as yours. Your hook is made out of an ox bone. He said that was the best kind, but sheep was all he had. It feels pretty sharp. I can hardly wait to try it out."

Before Jalon could get situated and get his hook baited and into the water, something awful happened. The river turned blood red and started stinking. Instantly, dead fish, turtles and frogs were floating everywhere.

The boys jumped back as fast as they could. Mecho was so shocked, his fishing pole and his left leg went into the river before he could catch his balance. The boys looked at each other in disbelief.

Terrified, Jalon snatched up his fishing pole and his two buckets. "Look at that! The river has turned into blood. This is scary. We better go tell everybody."

Mecho started to grab the bucket containing his two fish. To his horror, the water in the bucket had turned to blood as well. He dumped the contents out on the ground and threw the bucket as far away as he could. "We better get out of here. We need to go to your house and tell your mom first. My folks are both in town this morning. Nobody is going to believe this, you know? We'll have to bring them here to see for themselves."

When the boys arrived at the home of Jalon they were in for another surprise. All the water in the clay wash tubs and all the water in the house had also turned to blood. Jalon went into the house and found his mother standing at the kitchen table. She was crying uncontrollably. Between breaths she wailed, "Supper is ruined, and our clothes are ruined."

All the clothing the family owned, that they weren't wearing, was in the wash tubs floating in blood. The lamb roast she was preparing for their evening meal was in the same disgusting condition. Jalon looked at Mecho, who was silently staring at them, as if he was still in shock. Jalon put his arms around his mother and whispered, "What's happening, mama? The Nile River has turned into blood too."

Jalon was still hugging his mother when his father came dashing into the house. Mr. Grossman had been forced to leave work early when the water he was using to make bricks suddenly changed into blood. Since he was working just a short distance downstream from where Pharaoh and his servants were gathered, it did not take him long to find out what had happened.

When David realized the magnitude of the problem, he hurried home to his family as quickly as possible. Seeing the condition his wife was in when he arrived made him thankful he had hastened home. After his wife had calmed down considerably, Mr. Grossman had everyone sit down. "Let me tell you how all this mess came about."

"Apparently Moses and Aaron went to the river to find Pharaoh. When they found him, they approached the king unannounced again. Another

request was made that Pharaoh let us go worship our God. The three of them got into a big argument and they all started shouting. Just when Pharaoh thought he had the last word, Moses told his brother to strike the water of the Nile with his walking stick. Aaron did, and the river instantly turned to blood. Wanting to prove that was not a difficult task, Pharaoh called for his magicians. They used their enchantments to show Pharaoh they could turn water into blood too. Plus, as if that wasn't enough, Aaron stretched his rod over the streams, ponds and pools, causing *them* to turn to blood. Can you believe it? Every drop of surface water in all of Egypt has turned into blood. It didn't seem to make any difference if the water was inside the houses or out. At every place I passed on the way home the people were out in their yards. They were furious about the blood and the awful smell."

Mr. Grossman started for the door. "We need to clean this place up and get rid of this horrible smell. We also need to get some fresh water right away. On my way home I saw the Egyptians digging new wells. Evidently all that water is okay."

"I'll dig a hole out back so we can bury all this blood. Jalon, you and Mecho help me by bringing everything you can carry to the hole. Don't forget the water trough in the stable. You will need to bail that out. We will empty all this mess and bury it to keep the smell down."

"Then, we need to load all our pots and buckets on the ox cart and go get some good water. The Egyptians were giving water away to everyone that had a stone jar or clay pot. Mecho, we'll stop by your house so you can gather several containers and take some fresh water to your folks as well."

Chapter 3

A full week had passed since Jalon and Mecho had been to the Nile to do any fishing. They had gone to the river several times to check on the condition of the water but had left their fishing poles at home. Having the water turn into blood before their very eyes had been such a traumatic experience, the boys wanted to be certain the water was normal again before baiting a hook.

On the eighth day after the water and blood incident, Jalon was visiting in the home of his friend Mecho. The boys were trying to be creative and think of something fun to do, but they weren't being very successful in their pursuit. Finally, Mecho inquired, "Mom, do you think the water is safe for me and Jalon to go fishing?"

Ischa Poriah felt sorry for her son and his friend. She knew how much they dearly loved to fish. She also knew the odds of them catching any fish were slim to none. "Son, it is highly unlikely there are any fish left in the river. Remember, they all died just last week when the water turned into blood? I know how anxious you are to go fishing, but it's going to take quite a while for the current to bring an abundance of fish into the Nile again. You must be patient."

Seeing the disappointment on the face of Mecho, his mother quickly added, "However, I see no reason to keep you from your favorite sport. Seeing the pleasure you gain from just being on the bank of the Nile gives me joy as well. Yes, you may go fishing, but first, I want you to clean your room. We're expecting company this evening, and I need your help to make the house look nice."

The boys were so excited they quickly ran to the room Mecho shared with his brother, Ketar. They started shoving things back into the places where they belonged. While looking under the bed, Jalon noticed a live frog. Just as he was about to grab the critter, he heard a blood-curdling scream from inside the bedroom of Zina, the little sister of Mecho.

Her cry for help brought Ketar, Jalon and Mecho to her room in a flash. All three boys appeared at her door at the exact same time. They found Zina sitting in the middle of her bed shrieking, with frogs hopping all around her. The very moment they were prepared to rescue Zina, they heard Ishca screaming from the kitchen area.

Ketar grabbed his little sister and they all dashed to the kitchen. As they arrived at the doorway, they stared in disbelief at the sight of frogs hopping around everywhere. One was even sitting right in the middle of the bread dough. Ketar handed Zina to his mother and picked up the straw broom. He started sweeping the frogs outside. In just two or three strokes of the broom, a large heap of frogs piled up just outside the door. Jalon and Mecho started picking up frogs and throwing them outside. The more they tried to shoo the frogs out, the more the frogs came in. Soon, there wasn't even a place to sit down without sitting on a frog.

Jalon began wondering if the frogs were at his house too. Then he thought of his mother and the fact that she may be home alone. Jalon decided it was time for him to go. He didn't even take the time to tell Mecho and his family goodbye. He started running as fast as he could toward home.

All the way to his house Jalon dodged frogs by the thousands. He had squashed so many he had lost count. To his dismay, Jalon found the same horrible frog problem at his house as he did at the home of his friend. At least this time his dad was there.

Jalon had often seen a frog or two near the Nile while he was fishing, but he had never seen so many at one time. Nor had he seen them so far from the river. As Jalon pondered the image of having to contend with the frogs forever, he suddenly had another thought. "Dad, is this another plague? Do you think God did this on purpose? Like when He turned the water into blood?"

"Yes son, that's exactly what has happened. God sent another plague because Pharaoh is being stubborn. He has hardened his heart again. Pharaoh has refused a third request from Moses to let our people go worship God. God has sent another plague to show Pharaoh who's really in control. He may be king of Egypt, but God controls the king."

By now, the people of Egypt were beginning to wonder if *anyone* was in control. It was starting to dawn on the Egyptians that every time Moses and Aaron went to see Pharaoh it meant trouble for them.

Word was quickly spreading that Pharaoh had angered the God of the Hebrew people. Soon everyone knew the frogs that were keeping them confined in their homes were another plague sent by the God that Moses was talking about.

By coincidence, Mr. Poriah happened to be at the palace just as the frogs were starting to take over. He finished his business there and hurried home.

When Mr. Poriah arrived at his house, he observed his wife and children desperately trying to remove hundreds of frogs from the kitchen area, with mounds of injured ones just outside the door. He told everyone there was no way to get rid of the millions of frogs that were covering their land like a blanket. Mr. Poriah knew they should be using their energy to figure out how to cope with the problem rather than fighting against it.

Quickly taking charge of the situation, Mr. Poriah had his family sit down in a circle in the corner of a bedroom with everyone facing inward. That gave them some protection from the invasion of frogs. When everyone was seated he told his family, "I don't know how this will end, but I saw it all begin."

The brain of poor Mr. Poriah was so muddled he could hardly keep his thoughts and his speech coming at the same time. Mecho moved a little closer to his father. He scooted as close as he could get without sitting on his lap. Mecho didn't want to miss a single word of what his dad was about to say.

Mr. Poriah cleared his throat and began again, "Moses and Aaron came back to the palace to see Pharaoh today. They asked him to let the children of Israel go out into the wilderness to worship their God, but for the third time, Pharaoh refused."

"That made Moses mad, so he and Aaron left in a huff. When they got outside, Moses told Aaron to stretch his rod over the streams, rivers and ponds. This time, that action caused all these frogs to come up out of the water."

"When Pharaoh saw what was happening he got in a huff too. Then, not to be outdone, Pharaoh turned to his magicians and ordered them to do the same thing. They used their enchantments and brought up *more* frogs."

"Just before all of that started happening, the palace was immaculate, as usual. There was not a piece of dirt or a frog anywhere to be seen. Suddenly, I saw them coming. Thousands of frogs were hopping over each other trying to get inside. Almost instantly, frogs were ankle deep in the halls and in all the chambers of the palace." Snickering now, Mr. Poriah continued, "I didn't see this, but one of the guards told me some of the frogs jumped up into the lap of Pharaoh."

"Pharaoh was so horrified he jumped right off of his throne. The guard also told me it was impossible to keep the frogs away from the throne area. Pharaoh kept shouting and ordering the guards to remove the frogs, but there was nothing they could do. Finally, in a fury Pharaoh ordered Moses and Aaron back to town. When the two brothers got back to the palace and appeared before him, Pharaoh instructed Moses to pray to his God that He would take away the frogs. Moses simply asked, 'When do you want these frogs to be gone?' Pharaoh yelled, 'Ask God to remove the frogs tomorrow.' Having all those frogs in his lap must have softened Pharaoh, because he agreed to let the Hebrew people go sacrifice to their God if the frogs were gone by tomorrow."

Ishca jumped to her feet as she shouted, "Tomorrow?! Why not right now?! If I have to live with these frogs until tomorrow, I believe I'll croak. Pharaoh must be losing his mind. I sure would like to give him a piece of mine!"

Mecho hurried to his mother and gave her a reassuring hug. Mr. Poriah encouraged his family to stay huddled together. They would make it through this night, and things would be better in the morning. The family decided to skip supper and go right to bed. They all slept in one room, trying to frog proof it as much as possible.

Needless to say, everyone spent a sleepless night with the frogs. There was no relief. Every home had been invaded with thousands of them. It seemed that for every frog they threw out, two came in.

Sure enough, at the sight of dawn, dead frogs could be seen everywhere. The people quickly swept their houses and heaped the frogs into mounds outside. The smell was almost unbearable. People were grumbling throughout all of Egypt, saying they didn't know which was worse, the smell of the dead frogs or the smell of the blood from the week before.

The Egyptians didn't know it yet, but Pharaoh had hardened his heart as soon as he saw the frogs disappear. He again refused to let the Israelites leave Egypt and spare his people from any more plagues.

Chapter 4

With the frogs gone, things were just about to get back to normal in Egypt. Jalon and Mecho had not seen each other in several days. One pretty sunny morning, Jalon asked his mother if he could go fishing again. Mrs. Grossman struggled with her answer. She was torn between letting her son do what he loved the most and keeping him home where he would be safe. No one knew what might happen next, or when it would occur. Leah was a little apprehensive for Jalon to be out alone at such an unsettled time. She finally agreed as long as his friend Mecho had permission to go with him.

Jalon grabbed his cane pole and ran all the way to the home of his fishing buddy. After spending so much time apart, the boys were thrilled to see each other. Seeing his friend standing there with his fishing gear was too much. Mecho eagerly rushed to his mother and asked if he could go to the river with Jalon to do some fishing. Ishca gave her permission, with one big stipulation. They were not to bring home a frog or anything that resembled a frog.

Mecho hurried to the stable and snatched up his cane pole. Latching onto a wooden bucket as he came out the door, he was ready to go. Mecho always traveled light when he went fishing. He wanted to keep his hands free to carry home all the fish he caught. There would be plenty of bugs and worms near the river, so bait would not be a problem.

The day seemed perfect. Even though the boys had not caught a single fish all afternoon, they were having a great time relaxing in the shade and discussing all that had happened in the past two weeks. They agreed that it was not exactly fun, but it sure did make things exciting. All at once, both boys felt something biting them. They started itching all over their bodies, even on their heads.

Jalon squealed, "We must have sat on an ant hill or something! Come on, we can jump in the water and get these things off of us." One after the other, the boys leaped into the river. The coolness of the water took away the irritating itch. Jalon and Mecho played in the water for quite awhile. They were having so much fun they quickly forgot about the bites, but the relief was short lived. The minute they came out of the water the itching began again.

The boys soon had welts all over their bodies from scratching the bites. Before they had time to even gather up their fishing poles, Mecho shouted that he couldn't see. Turning to look, Jalon gasped in shock when he saw the eyes of his friend. They were swollen completely closed. Mecho had so many bites on his face he was almost unrecognizable. Leaving the fishing poles, Jalon helped his friend home before continuing on to his house.

When the boys arrived home, they learned they had not sat down on an ant hill as they had thought. They had lice, and so did everyone else in all of Egypt. In a very short time the people were distraught from the misery of scratching. Their entire bodies were red and swollen. Some already had raw sores.

The lice were also biting the animals. They had sores all over their bodies as well. Because of their discomfort they were becoming wild and uncontrollable. Some of the horses and cattle stampeded. The cats and dogs would not quit yelping and screeching.

The Egyptians were starting to catch on that this was another plague and guessed its probable cause. Some of the more vocal ones in the crowd said, "It must be from the God of those Hebrews again. Pharaoh should just throw them out of here so we can have some peace."

The Egyptians were right. The plague of lice *did* come from the God of the Hebrews. Moses had instructed Aaron to strike the ground with his rod. This time, the dust became lice throughout all the land of Egypt. Pharaoh became angry when his magicians tried, but failed to produce lice with their enchantments.

Pharaoh continued to harden his heart against the Israelites. He refused to let them leave Egypt to worship their God. After all, he was the Pharaoh. He was in control of what those Hebrews did. At least, that is what he thought.

Chapter 5

Mecho and his friend Jalon were distressed to see the effect the lice plague had on their pets. They were both raising prize animals for the fall festival that year. Mecho had a two thousand pound steer that he was sure would win the blue ribbon for the second year in a row. Jalon was raising a Fat-tailed Sheep as his trophy. It was only a lamb right now, but by the time of the festival it would be full grown. Both boys pampered and cared for their animals daily. It made them sick to see how their beloved pets had suffered from the lice. They were both glad the festival was still several months away so they could have time to re-groom and fatten their entries.

One day, while Jalon was visiting at the home of Mecho, the boys noticed swarms of flies. The flies were all over the prize steer Mecho was brushing. To calm the animal down, the boys took warm water with soothing spices and bathed the bites. Their effort did very little good. The flies kept coming and kept biting, until the bull soon became uncontrollable. The flies were also biting the boys. They were getting so bad Jalon and Mecho could not stay outside any longer. Just to walk the short distance to the house, they had to keep their mouths closed and hold their hands over their noses so the flies would not go down their throats.

It wasn't much better in the house. Everyone in the family was swatting flies. They were using anything they could grab hold of. Mrs. Poriah was using her shawl. Her husband had a handful of palm stalks. Mecho noticed his brother, Ketar, was using his sandal, and little Zina was smacking at them with a piece of cloth.

A fear for the welfare of his family came over Jalon. He announced that he had to go home immediately. Ishca was so frightened she didn't want Jalon to leave the house. Mrs. Poriah was afraid he wouldn't make it home safely. Jalon insisted that he must go home to see about his folks. He also didn't want his mother to worry about him. Ishca did not want Jalon to go outside since the flies were swarming to the point of blackening the sky. When Jalon kept insisting she finally agreed, but only if he would wear a cloth over his face and let Mr. Poriah go with him. They each covered their face with a cloth and ran the half mile distance to the Grossman home. As they put their feet down to cross over the narrow road where the land of Goshen began, they noticed there weren't any flies, not even one. Jalon was instantly relieved to know that his mother had not been suffering from those nasty insects.

Jalon excitedly told his mother about the fly plague in the other part of Egypt. Leah insisted that Ramar go get his family and bring them back to stay there until the flies were gone. Mr. Poriah promptly accepted her kind offer and quickly ran back home to rescue his wife and children. It seemed like an hour before Mecho and his family arrived but it was actually much shorter. It had taken a little longer because Mecho insisted on bringing his prize steer. The boys put the steer in the shelter with the lamb that Jalon was raising.

A short time later, Mr. Grossman came home. He couldn't work because of the flies. "I heard someone say there were no flies in Goshen. It seemed too good to be true, but I'm so glad to see that it is." The two fathers talked about what was going on and how long they thought it would last. David informed Ramar, "You know, these plagues are going to keep coming until Pharaoh agrees to let us go worship God."

Mr. Poriah squirmed in his seat. "Yes, I know. I just hope Pharaoh comes to his senses before Egypt is destroyed or we're all dead." Mrs. Grossman stepped closer to her husband. She put her hand over her heart. "I just thought of something. We must hurry and make beds of straw in the stable. When the Egyptians can no longer stand the plague of flies, some might bring their children here for safety. We must help as many as we can."

Meanwhile, back in Egypt, Pharaoh was among those who were still fighting flies. He finally had enough of the insects and called for Moses and

Aaron to return to the palace. As soon as they arrived, Pharaoh told them they could sacrifice to their God, but they had to stay in the land of Egypt.

Moses pointed out that the Egyptians would think it was an abomination if they saw the Hebrew people sacrificing animals they idolized. Moses looked straight at Pharaoh and shook his head 'no.' "Your people would be ready to stone us. No, we will go three days journey out into the wilderness and sacrifice there."

Pharaoh didn't like the sound of that. Of course, he did not like the constant fly swatting either. Pharaoh was thinking, "I'm thankful that I have servants to fan me. That does help to keep most of the flies away. The only problem is, they are still a nuisance, and I'm growing weary of all this." Finally, Pharaoh spoke. "I will let you go. Only, you are not to go very far away." Almost as an afterthought, he groaned, "Pray for me."

Moses assured Pharaoh he would pray and ask God to remove the flies. "The flies will be gone tomorrow." Then he added, "You'd better not be dealing deceitfully again. If you continue to harden your heart, God will continue to deal with you. Your trouble will not go away until you let the people of God leave Egypt."

The next morning, while Leah prepared breakfast for her guests, Mr. Poriah went home to see about the fly situation. When he came back, Ramar announced, "The flies are gone. I didn't see a single one, not even in the stable." As soon as breakfast was over, Mecho and his family thanked their hosts and left for home.

When Pharaoh observed that the last fly was gone, so was his good will. He changed his mind again. He hardened his heart and would not let the children of Israel go.

Chapter 6

Everyone in Egypt had their nerves on edge. They worried about what would happen to them next, especially when they saw Moses and Aaron walking toward the palace. The Egyptians knew that would mean trouble for them. They were tired of the plagues and were more than willing to have them stop, immediately.

One morning, after Mecho had spent the night with his friend, Jalon, the boys went out to the stable. Jalon wanted to brush the pet lamb he was raising for the fall festival. Jalon and Mecho were both getting really excited about the soon coming event. Both boys were certain they had the winning animal for their category.

Jalon had just started grooming his pet when Ketar came rushing into the shelter. Ketar was shouting that Mecho had to come home right away. When Ketar finally caught his breath and could speak clearly, Mecho found out his prize steer and three of the thoroughbred horses his father was raising, were all sick. Mr. Poriah had found them sprawled out in the stable and was unable to get any of them on their feet. Mr. Phalu, their nearest neighbor, was called upon to administer his special tonic but so far it had not taken affect. Ketar was sent to bring Mecho home so there would be an extra pair of hands to help take care of the sick animals.

Jalon ran into the house to explain to his mother what had happened and to ask permission to go to the home of his friend. Soon Jalon, Mecho and Ketar were all racing as fast as they could to the Poriah property.

The three boys arrived at the stable just as Mr. Phalu was pouring the second of two very large bottles of medicine down the throat of the bull. The helpful neighbor told the boys he would be back the next day. After giving detailed instructions on how to care for the animals, Mr. Phalu suggested that

Mecho and his brother stay up with the animals all night and give them several more bottles of the thick tonic.

Jalon stayed with his friends until it started to get dark. At that point he had to go home. In the meantime, Mecho and Ketar made up pallets of straw in the stable. With their beds situated across from the sick animals, they planned to take turns sleeping and taking care of the stock.

The next morning, Mr. Phalu came back as he had promised. He had been up all night. Animals all over Egypt were sick and thousands had died. The neighbor told Mr. Poriah, Mecho and Ketar, "I've been around animals and taken care of them all of my life, but I've never seen anything to compare with what has been happening in Egypt in the past two days. I was called to the palace during the night. Pharaoh has lost a lot of his chariot horses. About a fourth of his livestock is gone as well. The guards are saying Egypt is experiencing another plague. This time the epidemic is only affecting the animals. They are calling it murrain. The infected animals either get better or they die within twenty-four hours."

Mecho could see that his steer was very weak and wobbly but it was still alive. One of the horses had also made it and was able to stand for short periods of time. The other two horses were not as fortunate. They had died sometime during the night.

Mr. Phalu had only one bottle of tonic left. "I saved this bottle for your steer, Mecho. I was hoping he would be strong enough to survive. I know you have spent a lot of time keeping him healthy for the festival. I wanted to give him a fighting chance if I could. You can pour this last bottle of tonic down him later this afternoon. Hopefully that big guy will be much better by tomorrow." Mr. Phalu patted Mecho on the head and turned to walk back home.

That same morning, right after breakfast, Jalon ran to the home of his friend. He volunteered to watch over the steer and the remaining horse while

Mecho and his brother got some sleep. The animals were obviously still very sick, but they had made it until the second day. With constant care, hopefully they would soon be completely healthy again.

It took several days for the Egyptians to bury all the dead cattle, horses, donkeys, camels and oxen that had died during the plague of murrain. The children of Israel were grateful that God had again made a distinction between them and the Egyptians.

Chapter 7

Quite a few animals had died during the last plague of murrain. Mecho was thankful his steer had survived. Now he was kept busy trying to nurse it back to good health. Mecho had not seen his friend since Jalon had volunteered to sit with the animals the day after the plague struck. Mrs. Grossman didn't feel comfortable with Jalon being across town in the Egyptian neighborhood, so he was asked to stay close to home. Jalon occupied himself by doing his chores and grooming his lamb.

One pretty sunny morning, Jalon was especially lonely. He finished his morning chores and then just sat down on the back step. Mrs. Grossman watched her son. He had his head down, drawing in the sand with a stick. Her heart went out to the boy. Opening the back door, Leah suggested, "Son, how about if you go see Mecho today? Maybe he can go fishing with you. It will be good for both of you to get together and have some fun."

Jalon thought that was an excellent idea. He jumped up and gave his mother a big hug before racing to the stable for his cane pole. In a matter of a few seconds, Jalon was eagerly on his way to the home of his friend.

Unbeknownst to Jalon or his mother, God had sent another plague that very day. Moses had sprinkled furnace ashes toward heaven. As a result, boils broke out on man and beast alike. Since the plagues no longer affected the land of Goshen, the Hebrew people had no idea the latest plague had begun.

Excited and out of breath, Jalon arrived at the Poriah home. Eagerly, he knocked several times. Jalon thought it strange that no one was stirring. It was late morning, closer to lunchtime actually, and yet it seemed that the entire family was still in bed.

When Mecho finally came to the door, Jalon was shocked at what he saw. He knew it was his friend Mecho, but Jalon could hardly recognize him. Mecho had boils all over his face and body. He had several boils on his lips as well and could hardly speak through the tears. Mecho was in so much pain he had to talk without moving his lips.

It was really hard for Jalon to comprehend what Mecho was saying, but finally he understood. The whole family was covered with painful boils. They even had boils on the top of their heads and the soles of their feet. Mecho told Jalon he was glad he had come by and asked his friend if he would feed the steer and the one horse his dad had left.

When Jalon got to the animal shelter he was in for another shock. Even the steer and the horse were covered with boils. Both animals had lost a lot of weight. The horse looked like a baggy bundle of bones, and the steer was no longer of blue ribbon quality. Jalon fed and watered the animals, although they hadn't eaten what they had last been given. After cleaning up in the stable, Jalon headed for home.

Leah was surprised to see her son back so soon. After Jalon told his mother what had happened to his friend she sent him back to the Poriah home with homemade bread and chicken soup for the family.

Ishca thanked Jalon again and again for the food. Before Jalon left their home for the second time, Ramar Poriah asked him if he would turn the horse and the steer out into the pasture so they could fend for themselves.

Jalon didn't have the heart to tell Mr. Poriah the condition the animals were in. He simply did as he was asked. Jalon led the animals out to graze.

Jalon left the home of his friend that day with feelings of great sorrow. It made him sad to see Mecho and his family suffering so. Jalon silently wished Pharaoh would stop hardening his heart so the plagues would stop.

Chapter 8

It was getting more and more dangerous for Jalon to travel back and forth to the home of his friend, Mecho. Their Egyptian neighbors were becoming very hostile, throwing rocks and verbal accusations at every Hebrew they looked upon. The Egyptians were sick of the plagues. They wanted the Israelites to leave Egypt. The Hebrew people were quite ready and willing to leave, but Pharaoh still would not let them go.

Jalon and his mother continued to take food to the Poriah family and helped them with their domestic chores every morning. Jalon also took on the responsibility of the animals. Even though they were in the pasture, they needed some care. Jalon gave them water every day and brought them treats from home. He couldn't brush them because of the boils.

One evening, Jalon and his family heard the most violent thunderstorm they had ever known. It seemed to be coming in their direction. Jalon and his dad went outside to see what was going on. To their surprise, there was already a group of men gathered together to watch the downpour. The tremendous storm was very near, but it didn't seem to be moving any closer. The storm ended right at the dividing road between Egypt and Goshen. The amazed crowd could see fierce lightning illuminating the sky. It appeared that fireballs were running all the way to the ground. It was pouring down rain, with loud claps of thunder and huge hail coming down by the bucketful.

Jalon and his dad were soon joined by more Hebrew fathers with their sons. Everyone could see the hail piling up several inches deep all over the ground, but it was only on the Egyptian side. One man said, "I'm eighty-three years old and I have never seen such a violent storm in all my life." Another man agreed and commented on the size and quantity of hail that the storm was producing.

Mr. Grossman spoke softly to the crowd. "You know, all their flax and barley crops are ruined. I really feel sorry for all the innocent families that are suffering so much. Most of the Egyptians would have gladly given us permission to leave to worship God a long time ago. It's Pharaoh that is being so stubborn and hard-hearted."

The men that were listening fully agreed with him. One man remarked, "The Egyptians couldn't bring in their crops yesterday, but at least God warned them to stay inside and put their animals in a shelter."

Jalon started feeling a little sick. He hoped that Mecho and his family had heard the warning and heeded its message.

The storm raged on for quite some time. At the first sign that the violent assault had calmed in intensity, Pharaoh sent for Moses and Aaron. He admitted, "The Lord is righteous, and I and my people are wicked." Pharaoh quickly added, "Pray that God will stop the hailstorm, and then I will let you go, and you shall stay no longer."

Pharaoh was right; he *was* wicked. As soon as the storm ended he hardened his heart again and would not let the Hebrew people go. To him, it was a power struggle. He was the king, and he wanted to be in charge.

Just before noon the next day, Jalon and his mother left for the home of Mecho and his family. They were taking another basket of food and cleaning supplies. They planned to stay and help with the chores. The sky was still gray, but the storm had passed. As the two crossed into Egypt they had to wade through areas of ankle deep hail. Also, they had to dodge large puddles of water that were still covering the ground.

Jalon was glad his mother was with him. There was an eerie feeling in the air. There wasn't a single sound of anyone or anything stirring. They could see dead animals half covered with hail. It seemed like every cat and dog in the whole town had been killed. Trees and limbs were down in every direction. It was a very scary sight.

When Jalon and his mother eventually arrived at the Poriah residence, the scene was even worse. A large tree had fallen on their house, and all the chickens were dead and strewn about. Jalon started to cry when he saw the steer and the horse lying in a heap in the middle of the pasture. He knew immediately they were dead. Leah looked behind the house where their barley crop had been nearly ready to harvest. It was now lying limply on the ground half covered with hail. Any area that was not blanketed with ice was covered with large puddles of water.

Jalon knocked and knocked until Mecho finally opened the door. Jalon and his mother were surprised to find that the family was now living in only two rooms in the back of the house. It was the only part of the dwelling that had not been damaged by water. The entire household had a far-off, glassy kind of stare in their eyes. Everyone still had scars from the boils and none of them looked as if they had slept in weeks.

Mrs. Grossman could clearly see that food was not the only thing this family needed. They needed someone to take care of them, and they needed shelter. Leah offered both. She volunteered to take care of the entire Poriah family if they would only come to her house to stay, at least until they could get the tree and water damage repaired.

In a low voice, barely above a whisper, Mr. Poriah stated, "No, we're planning on moving our things out to the animal shed. The stable is warm and dry, and with no animals to care for, we can put down some fresh straw and make it fine."

Not being able to change the mind of Ishca or Ramar, Leah turned to leave the Poriah home. Grabbing the hand of her son as she walked out the door, Leah insisted, "I will send my husband over to bury your animals and to help you move your personal things to the stable." Ramar shook his head 'no.' "We appreciate all the help that you've given us, but it's getting far too dangerous for you and your family to be seen in this area. I fear that you may not even get back home safely today. You must leave now and not come back until it's safe. I'll send my oldest son to escort you home."

Mr. Poriah was right. The area was becoming a lot more violent. They had met several irate people on their way home. Mrs. Grossman was grateful Ketar had come along. She thanked him for helping her and Jalon get home safely.

As soon as Leah stepped foot inside her house, she burst into tears and cried uncontrollably for twenty minutes. Her heart was broken because she felt so sorry for those innocent people. By the time David returned home several hours later, Leah had gotten her emotions under control, but she was still feeling very sad. Leah ran to her husband and put her head on his shoulder. "If only Pharaoh would let us leave Egypt, all this pain and suffering would stop. Can he not see what he's doing to his people and to his country?"

Chapter 9

The days seemed to drag by for Jalon. Since he could no longer go see his friend Mecho, he seemed to have a lot of extra time on his hands. It was not safe for him to go to the river and fish either. The only thing Jalon had to help pass the time was his pet lamb. He kept grooming the lamb, even though it was highly unlikely they would be having the fall festival this year.

It was also no longer safe for Mr. Grossman and the other Hebrew men to leave the Goshen area. They couldn't work. Construction had stopped completely. The Israelites had no way to catch up on what was happening or what was about to happen. The only two men that dared to go near the palace were Moses and Aaron. Those two were in no danger because the Egyptians feared them as much as they did the plagues.

To compensate for their lack of information, the men of Goshen started having a bonfire meeting every night right after their evening meal. Moses and Aaron would join the meeting, answer any questions and let everyone know the latest word from God.

One evening Moses told the group, "The next plague God is about to send on Egypt is a swarm of locusts. Tomorrow God will send more locusts than anyone has ever seen on earth before. The locusts will eat every green thing that has been left alive in the land of Egypt."

The next day, Moses and Aaron marched themselves into the palace. They confronted Pharaoh with the fact that God was about to send a plague of locusts upon the land of Egypt. Unless he came to his senses and let the

children of Israel go worship their God, the locusts would come. When Moses was done with his speech, the brothers turned and walked out from Pharaoh.

    After Moses and Aaron left the palace, things really started buzzing. Pharaoh was enraged by the way he was being treated by those two Hebrews.

Not only Pharaoh, but his servants were also clearly distressed. The servants tried their best to talk Pharaoh into letting the Israelites go, but he would not budge. Pharaoh was almost delirious with anger. His servants finally suggested that he let only the Hebrew men go and serve God. The servants were quick to remind Pharaoh of the destruction that had already befallen their country.

After Pharaoh had time to calm down, Moses and Aaron were again brought before him. Pharaoh shouted, "Go, and serve the Lord your God." With another breath he demanded. "How many will be going with you?"

Moses informed Pharaoh, "Everyone will be going with us, young and old alike." Then Moses added, "We will also be taking our flocks and our herds."

Pharaoh shook his head 'no.' "Only the men will be allowed to go and serve the Lord." He was finished arguing. Pharaoh raised his hand and had the guards drive Moses and Aaron from his presence.

Moses went to the edge of town and lifted up his hand. He held his staff over the land of Egypt. God sent an east wind that blew the rest of that day and all that night. The next morning, the east wind brought the locusts. The insects were everywhere throughout the land, inside the homes and out. There were so many locusts the land was darkened by them. They stayed only on the Egyptian side of Egypt, not crossing into the land of Goshen.

As the Hebrew people looked from the land of Goshen to the area across Egypt, it was like looking into a war zone. Everywhere they looked there was total destruction. Most of the people shook their heads and sighed in anguish. Some cried in sympathy for the hurting Egyptians.

It wasn't long before Pharaoh sent an urgent message for Moses and Aaron telling them to come to the palace in haste. When they arrived, Pharaoh was visibly shaken. He lamented, "I have sinned against the Lord your God and against you." Then Pharaoh asked if they would forgive his sin just that once and seek their God, that He might remove this last plague.

Moses went out from Pharaoh and prayed that God would remove the locusts. The Lord sent a strong west wind, which took away all the locusts and cast them into the Red Sea. As the wind calmed, not one locust remained in all of Egypt. Again, Pharaoh did not keep his promise. He still wouldn't let the children of Israel go worship their God.

Chapter 10

Without going to see Pharaoh to warn him of another impending plague, the Lord told Moses to stretch his hand toward heaven so that a thick blackness would come over the land of Egypt. God was about to send a darkness so intense the people would be able to *feel* it. This time, the plague would last three full days.

As Moses lifted his hand toward heaven the light started to fade immediately. Moses hurried home before it got too dark to see his way. When he was safely outside the boundary of Egypt, Moses told the Israelites about the newest plague. He told them the thick darkness was only for the Egyptians. It wouldn't affect them in any way; they would still have light.

Just as in the plague of flies, murrain, boils, terrifying hailstorm and locust, the darkness plague stopped right at the very edge of the land of Goshen. The children of Israel could see the blackness over the land of Egypt. Some of the people went right to the edge of the road that divided the two lands so they could get a better look. The Israelites could feel the heavy darkness. It felt frightening just standing next to it.

It was not only dark in Egypt. It was *intensely* dark. The Egyptians could not even see someone standing right next to them. All the people of Egypt were frightened to the point of being terrified. They huddled in their beds, afraid to move for three days.

After the darkness finally lifted, Pharaoh called for Moses. Pharaoh informed him the Hebrew people and their children were free to go serve their God, but their flocks and herds must stay in Egypt.

Moses explained to Pharaoh again that the children of Israel must take their flocks and herds. The animals were needed for sacrifices and burnt offerings to their God. Moses stated, "Not a hoof shall be left behind."

Pharaoh wasn't used to anyone disobeying his commands. Usually, if someone talked back or disobeyed his orders they were executed. Pharaoh was furious with Moses. Nevertheless, he didn't know what to do with him. Pharaoh thought for a long time. Finally, he told Moses to leave his presence. He never wanted to see his face again. Pharaoh yelled, "The day you see my face again you will die!"

Moses was getting tired of Pharaoh lying to him. He became just as irate as Pharaoh. Moses shouted back in the same fierce tone, "You have spoken well, because I will never see your face again."

Moses left the palace without looking behind him. He was in a hurry to get back to the children of Israel. He had to tell the people to start packing. As soon as he stepped foot in Goshen, Moses called a special meeting. He told everyone to get ready. They were going home!

Moses declared, "Before long, these people will be begging us to leave." He informed the Israelites not to be afraid of the Egyptians any longer. Moses encouraged them to go borrow all the gold and silver jewelry they could possibly get, along with any other valuables they would like to take with them on their trip.

When the cheering finally died down, Moses advised the Israelites there would be one last plague across the land of Egypt. "This time," he warned, "we have something we must do to keep the plague from coming upon us." Moses instructed the children of Israel that they were to kill a lamb for their final meal in Egypt. The lamb must be without blemish and not yet a year old. If their family was too small for a whole lamb, they were to share it with their closest neighbor.

Moses cautioned, "Listen carefully. You are to take a hyssop branch, dip it into the blood from the lamb and put it on the top and the two side posts of your door. Then, everyone is to stay inside their house until morning. God is going to pass through Egypt at midnight tonight. At every home that doesn't have the blood on the door, the firstborn will be slain."

Jalon thought of Ketar, the older brother of his friend Mecho. He wished there was some way Ketar could be spared. Jalon shared his fear with his mom and dad. Time was very important. Mr. and Mrs. Grossman decided Jalon and his dad must go and talk with the Poriah family, while Leah went to borrow items from the Egyptians. They all left immediately.

Mr. Grossman gave permission for Jalon to run on ahead. He would be right behind him at a somewhat slower pace. Jalon took off running as fast as he could go to the home of his friend.

When Jalon arrived at the temporary dwelling of the Poriah family, things had changed. They were no longer warm and friendly toward him. Mr. Poriah held on to the stable door and blocked Jalon from seeing around him. He wasn't invited inside, and Mecho couldn't go outside. Jalon tried to explain about the impending danger for the firstborn of Egypt, but Mr. Poriah asked him to leave and closed the door.

Jalon was crying as his dad arrived at the building. Mr. Grossman instructed Jalon to knock again. This time, Mrs. Poriah answered the door and invited them inside their makeshift home.

Jalon stopped crying and tried to take deep breaths. Mr. Grossman wasted no time in telling the distressed family about the final plague God was about to send on Egypt. He explained how this plague would take the life of the firstborn of everyone in Egypt. Every household would be affected unless they did as God required. David then invited everyone to come to his house and avoid any further pain. He told how there would be safety under the blood, but they must take action without delay, because tomorrow it would be too late.

Silence reigned for several minutes, in which no one moved or seemed to take a breath. Mr. Grossman silently prayed that the family would make the right decision. To Jalon, it seemed like an hour had dragged by. Finally, Ishca burst into tears. Turning toward her husband, she gasped, "Surely you see the hand of God in all these plagues we've suffered. If we don't do what the God of the Hebrews requires, we will lose our boy. That would be more than I could endure."

Mr. Poriah listened thoughtfully as his wife spoke. After another few minutes he shook his head 'yes.' "Yes, you're right. We must obey the God of the Hebrews. We will go to Goshen and put ourselves under the protection of the blood on the doorposts, and Ketar will live."

Jalon had mixed emotions. He was happy that his best friend and his family would be safe, but he was sad for all the sorrow that would fall on the

Egyptian people later that evening. After returning home, Jalon had a long talk with his dad about all the deaths that would occur in Egypt that night.

Mr. Grossman told Jalon he was learning hard lessons early in life, but there were some things that man could not change. He needed to be strong, look ahead to the promises of God and not look back. Jalon knew his father was right, but it was indeed a hard lesson.

Later, Jalon had another talk with his dad. This time it was his father who brought up the subject matter. Mr. Grossman asked Jalon how he felt about parting with his lamb. He pointed out how the family needed to kill a perfect lamb for their dinner that evening, one without a single blemish. Jalon was aware that the only animal his family owned that fit the required description was the pet lamb he was raising. Jalon quickly determined that his lamb was the one that needed to be offered.

Jalon was growing up. He felt good that he had been able to raise a perfect lamb, one that could be given so his family and friends could be saved on their last night in Egypt. There would be other lambs but this one was needed at this time.

At sunset, David Grossman called a meeting in his home. The meeting included his family, the Poriah family and two of their closest Hebrew neighbors who were also spending the night. Mr. Grossman explained how the evening and their meal would proceed. Looking directly at Mr. Poriah, David stated, "Ramar, you and your family are truly welcome to stay in our home and under the safety of the blood. However, you will not be allowed to partake of the Passover meal, since you and your family are not Israelites." Mr. Grossman continued, "The Hebrew Nation is about to celebrate our very first

Feast of Unleavened Bread. The feast must be fulfilled exactly as God has commanded and only a true Israelite can participate. I want you to know that no one will go hungry. You and your family will be served from other food in the house."

Ramar Poriah assured his host, "My wife and I are grateful just to have our family safe for tonight. We're thankful your family cared enough to advise us of the upcoming danger. It will be a long and dreadful night. The fact that you welcomed us into your home is enough."

As frightened as the members of the Poriah family were, they were not thinking about food right then. Everyone had suffered so much from all the other plagues, they were afraid of going through another one. If this night passed without tragedy they would leave first thing in the morning to go back to their home. If their family made it through the night intact, they would ask for nothing else.

Chapter 11

It was past midnight but still dark when cries were heard all over Egypt. There was not a single house in all of Egypt where there wasn't at least one dead. Weeping could be heard in every dwelling, from the home of Pharaoh, to the homes of the servants. Even the prisoners in the dungeons were not spared. The firstborn of the cattle were slain as well.

All of Egypt was awake and stirring around. Mr. Poriah suddenly became afraid of what Pharaoh might do to them if he found out where his family had spent the night. He stood and announced that it was time for them to leave.

Before the Poriah family left his home, Mr. Grossman spoke privately with his guest. "Ramar, bring your family back here and stay in this house after we're gone. It will be much more comfortable than living in the stable. At least live here until you get the repairs done to your place."

Mr. Poriah hugged his dear friend. "You know, I think I'll take you up on that offer. As soon as the shock wears off, everyone will want property in Goshen. Egypt is pretty much destroyed. Besides, living in this house will remind me and my family what good people lived here before us."

Mr. and Mrs. Poriah had tears of gratitude flowing from their eyes as they hugged their friends and said goodbye. Jalon and Mecho were tearful as well. They knew they would never see each other again, but at least everyone was safe.

At the palace, Pharaoh was so distraught his servants were afraid to enter his presence. They came trembling when they were summoned. One of the servants was hastily dispatched to Goshen with orders to bring Moses and Aaron back to the palace as quickly as possible.

Everyone in the land of Goshen was ready to leave Egypt for good. They were delighted when Pharaoh called Moses and Aaron to the palace. It was so early in the morning it still seemed like night when Pharaoh gave the order. He commanded Moses, "Take your flocks and your herds as you have said, and go." Then, very unexpectedly, Pharaoh added, "Bless me also."

The children of Israel were relieved to be on their way out of Egypt. After all those years of captivity, they would not have to spend another day in Egypt. Likewise, the people of Egypt were delighted that the Hebrews would be gone soon. The Egyptians couldn't have them leave fast enough. They gave the Israelites everything they needed and wanted hoping to get rid of them quickly.

It was not just the adults that were soliciting things. The children were boldly asking too. Mr. and Mrs. Grossman told Jalon he had their permission to ask the Egyptians for some items for himself. In no time at all, Jalon had three small feed sacks full of rings, coins, gold nuggets and marbles. Jalon felt as rich as Pharaoh. He'd never had so many treasures in his entire life.

While the Israelites were scampering around collecting treasures from the Egyptians, Moses was organizing the procession that would soon leave Egypt. Moses thought the hardest part of the trip to the land of Canaan was getting Pharaoh to let the people go. It did not take very long for him to decide that had been the *easy* part.

Moses had six hundred thousand men, plus women and children, waiting to be led out of Egypt. They all had their household items, clothes, flocks and herds ready to take with them. The children of Israel had spent four hundred and thirty years in Egypt. Now they were leaving, and they were not coming back.

Jalon and his family weren't the first in line for the exodus, but their little, two-wheeled cart was very near the front. So many things were happening it was hard for Jalon to keep up with it all. He was raring to get going, and it seemed as if they never would.

The procession finally started moving. Moses was out in front, carrying nothing but a cloak and his rod. Aaron and Miriam were further back with a wagon loaded down with supplies.

One of the most important things that Moses made sure to take with him as he left Egypt was the bones of Joseph. Joseph had predicted, long years before, that this day would come to pass. Before he died, Joseph had requested that when the children of Israel left Egypt for the Promised Land they take his bones with them. As a teenager Joseph had been taken into Egypt against his will and sold as a slave, but he didn't want his remains to stay there. He wanted his bones to go back to the country where he was born. Joseph desired to be buried in the Land of Canaan, next to his family members: Abraham, Isaac and Jacob. Moses was determined to fulfill that request.

   Everyone was lined up and anxiously waiting for Moses to give the signal to proceed. Before the group started moving, Mr. Grossman warned Jalon not to wander off. He was to keep his family and their ox cart in sight at all times. Jalon couldn't believe how anxious he was to be leaving Egypt. This was a wonderful new day, the first of a wonderful new life in the Land of Promise.

Chapter 12

The Lord was leading the way for the children of Israel. He was taking them out of Egypt and into the Promised Land. He led with a pillar of cloud by day and a pillar of fire by night. The columns could be seen by everyone. When they finally stopped, their first camp site was next to the Red Sea.

As soon as Jalon and his family were out of the city limits of Egypt, away from the loud noises of the mobs, Mrs. Grossman suggested that Jalon lie down on top of their two-wheeled cart and get some sleep. Jalon had been awake for almost twenty hours. His body was exhausted, but he was too excited to sleep. He finally agreed to at least lie down and rest.

It was not quite daylight, so Jalon could easily see the fire from the pillar of the Lord in the dark sky. It comforted him to know that God was so near. It made him feel completely safe. Before Jalon could have another thought, he was fast asleep.

Meanwhile, back in Egypt, things were in an uproar. It didn't take very long for Pharaoh to regret his decision of ordering the Hebrew people out of his country. He realized the great loss to the workforce that Egypt would suffer with them gone. When he came to his senses, he ordered six hundred of his chosen chariots and captains, along with his entire army, to chase down the Israelites and bring them back.

Jalon slept peacefully for several hours. He knew nothing of the excitement going on around him. By the time he awoke, the entire Israel nation had exited Egypt and had set up camp next to the Red Sea. At first, Jalon thought he was having a wonderful dream, but as he became more awake, he realized his family was really moving out of Egypt. He was truly on his way to the land God had promised his people.

As soon as Jalon was fully awake, he heard a loud commotion coming from the crowd that was behind his cart. He climbed up and stood on the highest portion of the cart to get a better view. Jalon wanted to see what everybody was shouting about.

To his surprise, Jalon saw hundreds of horses and chariots, along with a huge cloud of dust heading their way. He was so disturbed by the sight he literally fell to the ground. He ran to tell his dad that the whole Egyptian army was after them.

Jalon was not aware of it, but his father had just come back from speaking with Moses. Mr. Grossman hugged his wife and son and told them not to be afraid. He shouted excitedly, "God has brought us this far. He will see us through. God always finishes what He starts." Mr. Grossman hugged his family again and repeated what Moses had just said to him. "Don't be afraid, the Lord will fight for us."

Jalon hurried to climb back on top of the cart. He could hardly believe what he was seeing. As Moses held his rod over the sea, a very strong east wind started blowing. In just a few minutes, Jalon could see the water dividing and making a split in the sea.

As Jalon watched, the water completely parted. At the same time, he saw a movement out of the corner of his eye. He turned just in time to see the fiery pillar of the Lord moving from in front of the Israelite camp to the back.

The angel of God, which went before the Israelites, moved and went behind them. The column now stood between the camp of the Israelites and the camp of the Egyptian army. The cloud made darkness for the Egyptians and light for the Israelites.

All of a sudden, Jalon had his attention brought back to the front of the camp. The people up ahead were going right into the midst of the sea. Jalon was so captivated, he shouted to his parents, "Look at that!"

Mr. Grossman instructed Jalon to hurry and climb down. Then, he quickly headed the ox and the little cart right toward the water. As Jalon and his family drew closer, Jalon could see there was a path right through the water. The ground wasn't muddy, but completely dry! There appeared to be a wall of waves piled up on each side of them. It seemed as if it was a mile wide. His dad was driving their cart right through the sea!

Jalon was almost too overwhelmed to speak, but finally he inquired, "Dad! Did this ever happen before?" His father laughed and said, "No son, this is a first. This is just a sample of the power of our God."

When Jalon and his family were safely across, they climbed up on a steep hill to observe the drama unfolding before their eyes. They watched as one by one, the Israelites walked or drove their carts through the opening to the other side.

Finally, the Lord gave the army of Pharaoh daylight again. They were determined not to let a single person get away. Pharaoh had given them orders to bring all the Hebrew people back to Egypt, and that was exactly what they intended to do. The Egyptian army took their horses and chariots and followed the Israelites right into the midst of the sea.

Jalon was amazed by the sight before him. As he stared intently, chariot after chariot lost its wheels and began dragging on the ground. "Look dad, there goes another one. The Egyptian army keeps having chariot pileups. They're not making much progress, are they dad?"

Mr. Grossman was cheering about the chariot mishaps just as loudly as Jalon was. Between cheers, he shouted, "You know son, the wheels coming off those Egyptian chariots is the hand of God too. God is slowing them down so our people can all get across without danger."

Jalon and his family continued their vigil until the last of the Israelites got safely through the opening in the water. They also watched as the Egyptian army was forced to leave their broken down chariots scattered along the way. The soldiers proceeded the best they could until they eventually maneuvered themselves to the center of the sea. Then, with one quick swipe, Jalon saw Moses jerk his hand down to his side. It was the same hand that had been holding the rod over the sea.

The wind instantly changed direction and the walls of water came crashing down. The path through the sea was suddenly gone. The waves completely covered Pharaoh's army in an instant. The Israelites watched in horror as everyone was buried under tons of water. There was not one survivor.

Shocked, Jalon shouted, "Wow! I sure am glad God is on our side, how about you dad?"

Mr. Grossman gave Jalon a big hug and declared, "Yes, I am son. Yes, I am."

About the Author

Carol Craven Bates resides in middle Tennessee but is originally from New Jersey. She enjoys reading, writing and sewing. Carol and her husband have two daughters, two sons and seven grandchildren. Through her stories, Carol hopes to encourage boys and girls to learn to enjoy reading. She chose Christian fiction so children would see how exciting the Bible is and how it fits into their everyday lives.

About the Illustrator

Janet ("Jan") Church Hopkins resides in Centerville, Tennessee, but is originally from a small town in West Virginia situated on the banks of the Ohio River. She is the mother of two grown children: Trista, a college student, and Andrew, a Specialist in the Ohio Army National Guard, who is married and has a new baby son.

Jan is a professional watercolor artist who believes that her talent is God-given and should be used to His glory. If you wish to contact her regarding her art, you may e-mail her at: jan@JollyJourneyPublishing.com. This is her first book illustration, and it is lovingly dedicated to her family and those special friends ("You know who you are") who have encouraged her to pursue her dream of using her talent for God and to make a difference in the world.

www.ingramcontent.com/pod-product-compliance
Lightning Source LLC
Chambersburg PA
CBHW041535240626

47164CB00002B/24